£6.75

THE DANDY
ANNUAL 2004

THIS BOOK BELONGS TO-

_____

_____

_____

_____

_____

© D.C. Thomson & Co., Ltd., 2003.
Printed and published by D.C. Thomson & Co., Ltd.,
185 Fleet Street, London, EC4A 2HS.
ISBN 0-85116-823-X

INDUSTRIAL
STRENGTH
RIVETS!

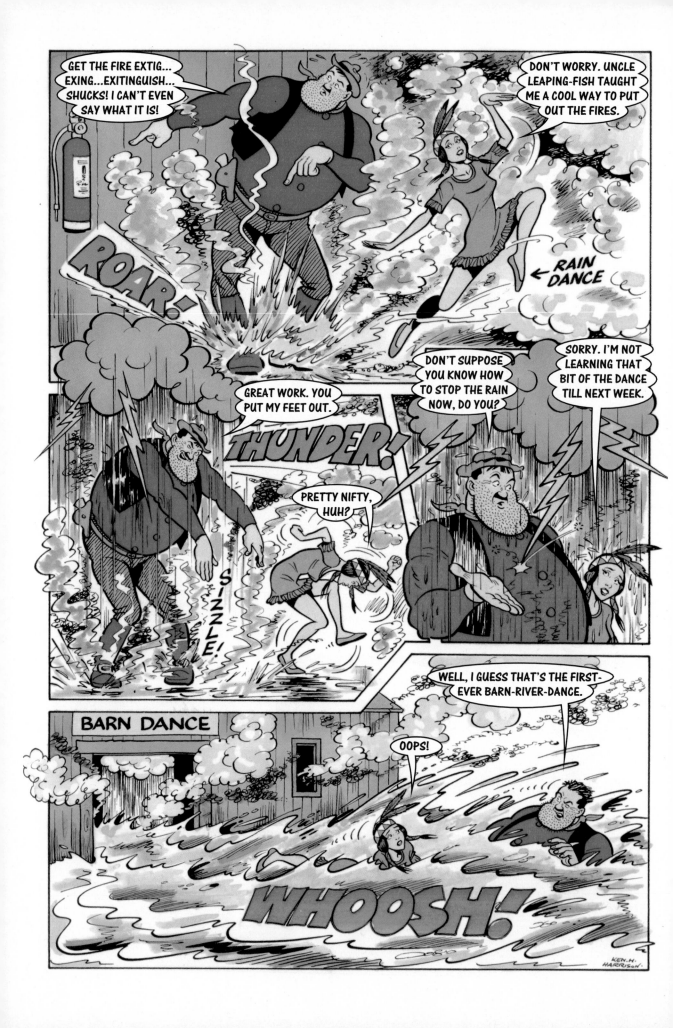

olliefliptrik@dandy.com

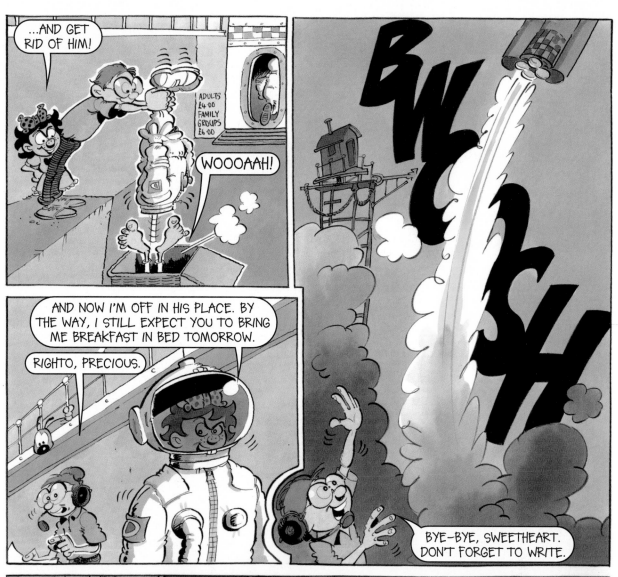

CASTAWAY
Conundrums

Poor old shipwrecked Alf is all alone on the desert island.

SPIDER
EARWIG
COCKROACH
BEETLE
MOTH
MOSQUITO
ANT
FLY

Bugs are the only company Alf has on his island. Can you find these bugs in the grid?

C	A	R	E	S	K	R	E	G
M	O	S	Q	U	I	T	O	S
A	F	C	E	L	N	O	G	P
A	S	L	K	A	N	I	B	I
T	P	E	M	R	W	F	R	D
Y	I	H	O	R	O	E	L	I
R	D	O	A	T	I	A	W	Y
B	E	E	T	L	E	T	C	O
C	R	L	Q	U	M	O	T	H

ACTAWSYA

The batteries in Alf's radio are running down. He heard his name but the rest of the message got a bit scrambled. Un-jumble the letters to find out what Alf was called.

Alf's SOS message has been thrown out to sea in a bottle. Can you find the path the bottle must take to find the rescue ship?

START

FINISH

WOOD

FIRE

Alf needs wood for his fire. Can you turn WOOD into FIRE by changing one letter at a time?

STEVE EARL

The metal maid scowls; no chance will she miss -
To pay back the joker who fixed her like this!

TIN LIZZIE

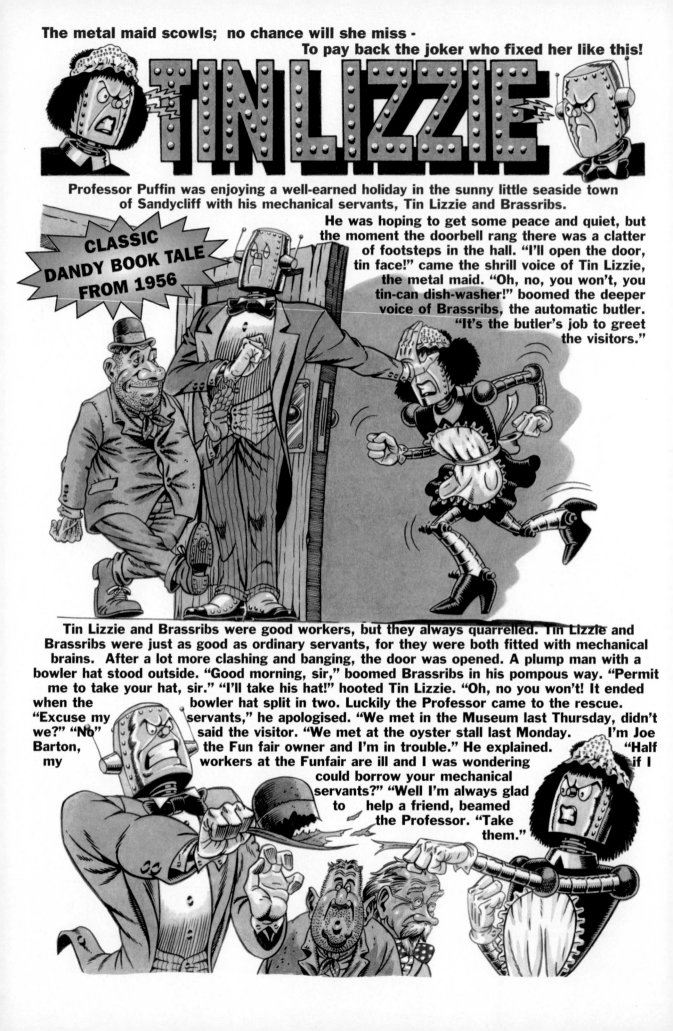

Professor Puffin was enjoying a well-earned holiday in the sunny little seaside town of Sandycliff with his mechanical servants, Tin Lizzie and Brassribs.

CLASSIC DANDY BOOK TALE FROM 1956

He was hoping to get some peace and quiet, but the moment the doorbell rang there was a clatter of footsteps in the hall. "I'll open the door, tin face!" came the shrill voice of Tin Lizzie, the metal maid. "Oh, no, you won't, you tin-can dish-washer!" boomed the deeper voice of Brassribs, the automatic butler. "It's the butler's job to greet the visitors."

Tin Lizzie and Brassribs were good workers, but they always quarrelled. Tin Lizzie and Brassribs were just as good as ordinary servants, for they were both fitted with mechanical brains. After a lot more clashing and banging, the door was opened. A plump man with a bowler hat stood outside. "Good morning, sir," boomed Brassribs in his pompous way. "Permit me to take your hat, sir." "I'll take his hat!" hooted Tin Lizzie. "Oh, no you won't! It ended when the bowler hat split in two. Luckily the Professor came to the rescue. "Excuse my servants," he apologised. "We met in the Museum last Thursday, didn't we?" "No" said the visitor. "We met at the oyster stall last Monday. I'm Joe Barton, the Fun fair owner and I'm in trouble." He explained. "Half my workers at the Funfair are ill and I was wondering if I could borrow your mechanical servants?" "Well I'm always glad to help a friend, beamed the Professor. "Take them."

Fairground Frolics

Half an hour later, Brassribs and Tin Lizzie were clanking along to the Funfair. It was already crowded and the music was blaring. Mr. Barton halted at one of the side-shows.

"This is the Fat Lady," he said to Tin Lizzie. "You take charge here. Yell as loudly as you can to attract customers."

"Leave it to me," replied the tin maid, and she climbed on to a platform and began bawling: "Walk up! Walk up! Only a quid to see the fat Lady! The greatest show on earth, folks! Walk up and see..." Tin Lizzie broke off, glaring, for her voice was suddenly drowned by an even louder bellow from a neighbouring tent. "Step this way for the Human Skeleton! The thinnest man in the world! Get your tickets now, ladies and gentlemen!"

Tin Lizzie snorted angrily. Right next door to her was Brassribs, running the Human Skeleton show with a voice like a foghorn.

Crowds gathered around as the mechanical servants tried to shout each other down!

Then a crafty gleam came into the butler's eyes. He nipped inside the booth and took a screwdriver from a tool chest.

"I'll fix that tin dishwasher!" he muttered as he crept along to the Fat Lady's tent and slipped inside. But Tin Lizzie spotted him. "What's the old villain up to now?" she muttered suspiciously?

She bounded through the entrance after Brassribs, but she didn't know the butler was waiting just inside. He stuck his foot out and the metal maid went sprawling.

Sitting in a chair in the middle of the tent was the Fat Lady. Brassribs tipped the chair over so that the Fat Lady shot out and sat down heavily on top of Tin Lizzie. "Help!" gasped the tin maid, pinned down by the enormous weight on her. With a rumble of triumph, Brassribs set to work on a small screw in Lizzie's neck.

"This will shut you up," he cackled. "I'll make scrap iron of you when I get up!" yelled Lizzie. "I'll..." her voice suddenly faded to a stuttering croak. "I'll m-m-m-make sc-sc-scrap... "

Brassribs ran from the tent, taking the tiny screw. It was part of the works that controlled Lizzie's voice. Now she couldn't shout. The only sound she could make was a wheezy stutter. "The old villian!" she gurgled in dismay. "He-s p-p-pinched my v-v-voice!"

"This way for the Human Skeleton!" blared Brassribs. With Tin Lizzie no longer able to shout him down, he was having everything his own way.

Furiously angry, Tin Lizzie was clanking towards the butler, when Mr. Barton came over. "Why aren't you doing any work?" he demanded. "I told you to shout." "I kik-kik-can't," Lizzie wheezed. "What?" yelled the man. "Speak up!" "I c-can't speak up," spluttered Lizzie. "Th-th-th-that b-b-brass-faced old pie-can has pinched m-my volume-control. "I don't want any trouble here," said Mr. Barton. "I wanted you to take over the job sword-swallower and fire-eater. But it's no use if you can't shout. I'll have to get the butler to do it." Tin Lizzie was left standing, glaring. She clanked off to a workman's hut to see if she could find a screw to replace the missing one. She was poking amongst a box of rusty old nuts and bolts when one of the fairground workmen came in. "Hey, you can't have those, they're for the sword-swallower's act. Swallowing old iron is part of his show." "Wh-wh-wh-what's in th-th-that other box?" croaked Lizzie, pointing. "You can't have anything out of that either," grunted the man. "That's the fireworks for tomorrow night when the fair closes."

ACME
FIREWORKS
COMPANY
DANGER!

Tin Lizzie's eyes gleamed craftily. She followed the workman to the stall where Brassribs was to perform and watched him put down the box on the platform. Lizzie immediately ran back to the hut where the fireworks were kept and grabbed a handful. Taking these, she ran back to the stall and scattered them among the old nuts and bolts.

Brassribs stood on the plaform, bawling hoarsely: "Walk up! The sensation of a life-time! I can swallow anything! Swords, fire, bits of red-hot coal, old iron - anything!" Brassribs picked up a long sword and poked it down his tin throat.

Then he turned to the box of rusty old nuts and bolts and stuffed handfuls into his mouth. "Now for the final sensation," boomed the butler. "Fire-Eating!"

Fire-Eating Fireworks

He snatched up a blazing brand and thrust it into his mouth. "The rest of the show will take place inside," he trumpeted. "Get your tickets now -"

A strange sizzling, rumbling noise suddenly sounded inside him. BANG! FIZZZ-ZZZ-ZZZ! WHOOOOOSH! A flash of flame and a shower of nuts and bolts shot from the butler's mouth, scattering the crowd in panic. Tin Lizzie chortled. The flame from the torch had started the fireworks exploding inside Brassribs. "Don't run away!" yelled the butler. "The show is just going to begin. Step up - "BANG-BANG! FIZZZ-ZZZ! WHOOOSH! He was firing showers of old iron at the crowd every time he opened his mouth. There was a wild rush for shelter. "We've seen all we want to see already," yelled one battered onlooker. He turned to run for cover, then fell flat on his face as a chunk of old iron hit him. "Ow! I'm shot!" he howled.

Mr. Barton came running over. "What are you trying to do" shouted at Brassribs. "That's Battling Bender you just bowled over. We won't have a boxing champ if he's hurt."

"I'm hurt already!" moaned Battling Bender. I quit!"

"All right!" yelled the angry showman, shaking his fist at Brassribs. "This is your fault! You'll have to take his place!"

The Boxing Booth Battle

Tin Lizzie hopped into the ring behind him. "C-c-come on then, f-f-fight!" she ordered. With a roar of rage Brassribs jumped up and slammed a punch at her. The tin maid ducked and put a dent in the butler's jaw with a right uppercut.

In fury Brassribs tore one of the corner posts from the boxing ring and whacked Tin Lizzie over the head with it. Lizzie replied by nipping out of the ring, grabbing one of the seats and smashing it over the butler's head.

In minutes the booth was wrecked and everyone had left. Mr Barton came dashing along and found tin Lizzie dragging Brassribs out of the wreckage by the collar. "I'm t-taking him h-home for repairs," piped Lizzie. "We'll b-b-be back l-l-later."

"Not if I know it," spluttered Mr Barton.

Professor Puffin soon had Tin Lizzie's voice put right and Brassribs' dents straightened out, but the two mechanical servants didn't go back to work at the Barton Funfair again - Mr. Barton took jolly good care of that!

CUDDLES *and* DIMPLES *in*
"THE PILLOW CASE"

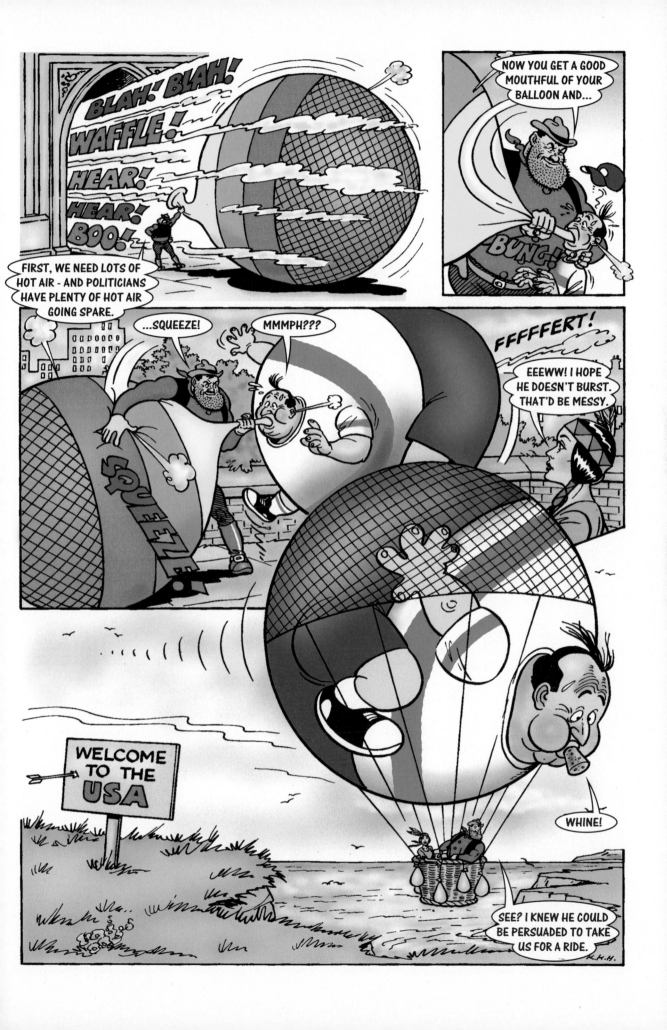

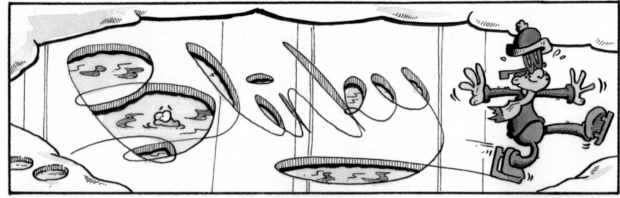

...P5? P5?

GLUBBA-LUBBA!

SPLAT!!

THIS IS BEST BEHAVIOUR?

SCOFF!

DARK CHOCOLATE

BUUURRRPP!

PINK SOFT TOFFEE

GUZZLE!

MUNCH!

LIQUORICE

RIGHT! I'LL SHOW THEM!

GOT YOU ALL!

YEEKS!

LET GO! THERE'S LOADS MORE TO DO HERE!

YANK!

YOWP!

Norman's Horrible HOMEWORK

Homework!
Don't you just hate It?

Isn't it a terrible word? Home-work. Break it down. It means working at home. But home's not for working. It's for having fun, playing games, watching telly, for fighting with your brothers and sisters and annoying your parents. Especially for annoying your parents. Why? Because they make you do homework, that's why.

There's nothing at all to recommend homework to anyone. But still parents make you do it. Why? Is it for your own good? They'll say it is. They'll say it's because they want you to become clever and get good jobs when you grow up? But is that the truth? Not bloomin' likely. It's because, while you're

locked away, your nose stuck in a book of boring maths problems - you know the sort of thing: "If it takes a man 5 hours to empty a bath full of water using a 500ml cup, how long would it take him to do it using a 300 ml tumbler?" The answer to the problem is, obviously 'Who cares?' or, alternatively, 'He took out the plug'. But anyway, while you're doing boring maths problems or even more boring spelling tests or geography so brainbogglingly boring you'd rather go to the dentist and have all your teeth taken out without anaesthetic, what are your parents doing? They're downstairs on the sofa, hogging the telly's remote control and laughing like tickled hyenas, that's what. Rotters.

But maybe your parents would think twice about making you do homework if they heard this story. You see, this is a story about homework going terribly, terribly wrong.

It begins with a nice little lad called Norman. A more ordinary boy you couldn't imagine. Normal Norman, some people called him. But then people like to give out nicknames like that, don't they? Anyway, Norman came back from school one day and was just hanging his schoolbag up on the banister when his Mum asked him: "Do you have any homework, Norman?" I ask you. The poor lad hadn't even had the chance to get his coat off and already the old trout was badgering him about homework. So did Norman get the chance to sit down and watch his favourite show on telly? Did he get to make himself a bit of toast or go out to play footy with his mates? Not on your nellie. He wasn't even in the door two minutes before his Mum had punted him off upstairs to do his homework. Wasn't it enough that he'd had to spend all day doing rotten school-work without doing more at home?

So, off poor Norman trudged, up to his bedroom to do his horrid, rotten, stinky homework. And didn't he have LOTS of it to do? The clock ticked around and around as he worked on. An hour doing daft sums he'd never need to use when he grew up because he had a calculator AND a computer. And then there was the dull book he had to read. And not just read. He had to write a report on it as well. And when that was out of the way, he had to read up on history. Why bother

reading about history of all things? If he ever wanted to know about olden days all he had to do was ask Grandad - he was so old that he'd lived through loads of history.

Eventually, after hours and hours of hard work, Norman was finished. He'd taken so long over the homework that he'd out-grown two sets of clothes. But at least he was finished. Norman was just stuffing all his books back into his school-bag when his poor little heart sank. Because sitting there at the bottom of his bag was another bit of homework. Another bit of blinkin', bloomin', flippin' homework!

And it wasn't just any old bit of homework. It was a science project. A science project he had to hand in first thing in the morning! What could he do? Build a table-top volcano? No, the last time he did that he'd used too much washing powder and cleaned out the whole school. So Norman hummed and hawed, sweated and strained, schemed and thought but for all his brain-bashing, poor Norman couldn't come up with a single idea for a science project. And so Normal Norman, the quietest kid in his class, flew into a terrible rage. He stamped his foot and bellowed the worst, rudest word he knew. "Aw, **BUM!!**" he shouted, And then he stomped around his bedroom, kicking his poor old teddy bear, Chuckles, out of the open window and throwing his favourite football against the wall with all his strength.

Of course, he had to dive out of the way to avoid getting smacked in the face as the football rebounded off the wall. Norman heard the ball THWACK off the wardrobe door and as he looked up from the floor, he saw his chemistry set teetering and tottering on the top of the wardrobe. He was just getting to his feet so that he could catch the chemistry set... when off it toppled, plunging to the floor where all the various test-tubes, jars and containers burst and broke, spilling all of the chemicals onto the carpet where they started to bubble and fizz, burble and bloop, turning into an ominous frothy mass, creeping towards him across the carpet. Being a clever lad, Norman did the only sensible thing he could: he screamed like a banshee with toothache and dived under the bed. Oh, he had to kick and shove old comics and toys and books out from under there to make room for himself, but he was sure that if anybody was going to be saved by the bed it was him. That was when his parents

burst into the room. They'd heard Norman's shriek and all the commotion and racket caused by the ball and the falling chemistry set. And while they were a bit worried about Norman, they were really mostly looking to tell him off for yelling "Bum!" so loudly. But when they walked into the room, guess what? They walked straight smack-bang into the middle of

the foaming, bubbling froth monster Norman had created.

"Now see here, Norman," Dad started to say, but his voice choked off as his face began to twist and contort, squish and squash. Hair started sprouting from all over his body. It sprang out of his ears, from up his nose and it fairly shot out from up his sleeves and trouser legs.

Mum opened her mouth to say something but all she could do was utter a loud "SQUAWK!" It took Norman a moment to realise that something was wrong because Mum tended to squawk a lot anyway when she came into his room. Usually a complaint about how messy it was. But this was different because now Mum had sprouted feathers from all over her head and body and her hands were turning into bird-like claws. She even had claws bursting through the toes of her slippers, which annoyed Norman a bit because he'd given her those slippers for Christmas last year.

Within minutes, Dad had transformed into a hairy, snarling beastie and Mum was some kind of exotic, plumed bird. "What'll I do with them now?" Norman thought to himself. And then he had a sneaky, sneaky thought. "I wonder..." he said.

The next day, Norman came out of school grinning a grin so wide it's a wonder the top of his head didn't topple off. He had come top of the class for his project - on the two strange

and mysterious animals he'd found and taken to school. Everybody had said "Oooh!" and "Aaaah!" and had asked questions about what the strange creatures were called and where Norman had found them. He'd made up the answers obviously - he didn't want everybody knowing that his parents were so weird - but nobody had caught him out and the teacher had patted him on the head and given him an A+.

That night, Norman sat at home, on the sofa watching telly and hogging the remote control to himself. His parents would never nag him to do his homework again. But of course, he would have to clean out their cage from time to time...

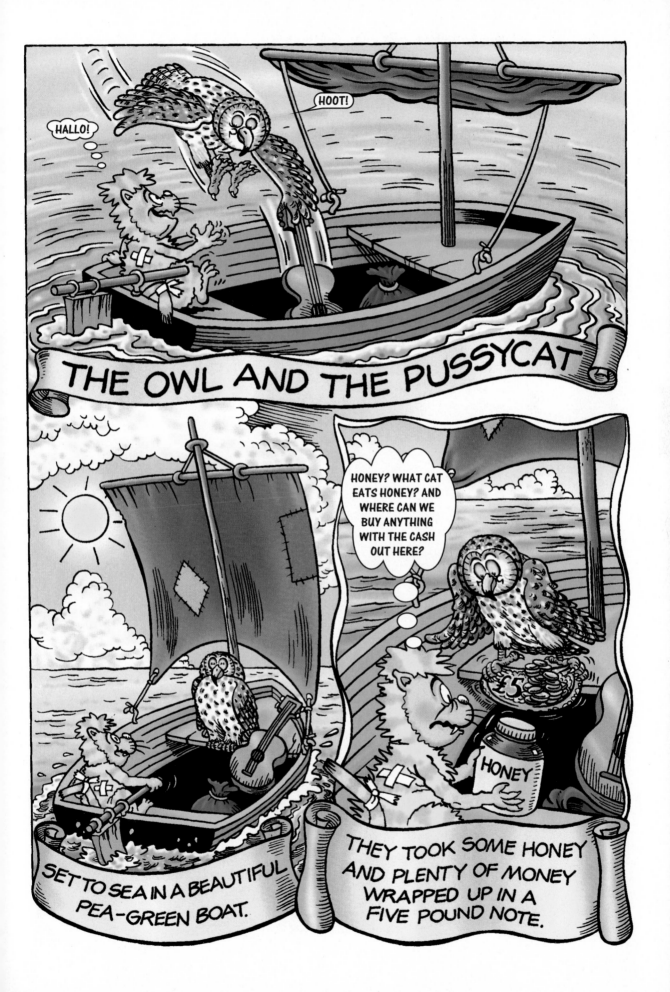

HMMM...
... THE OWL LOOKED UP TO THE STARS ABOVE
AND SANG TO A SMALL GUITAR...
...STUPID BIRD!
WIPE!
RUB!
SPLASH!
The softy editor would like to
point out that no sea-faring
owls were hurt or eaten during
the making of this story.

PARCEL FOR WINKER WATSON.

THAT'S ME!

YAHOO! IT'S THE NEW TOMB STEALER TEN GAME. UNCLE REG HAS SENT IT TO ME.

COOL!

I'LL HAVE THAT!

EH?

NEW COMPUTER GAME, EH, WATSON.

BOO! IT'S FANSHAW OF THE FIFTH FORM. WHAT A BULLY.

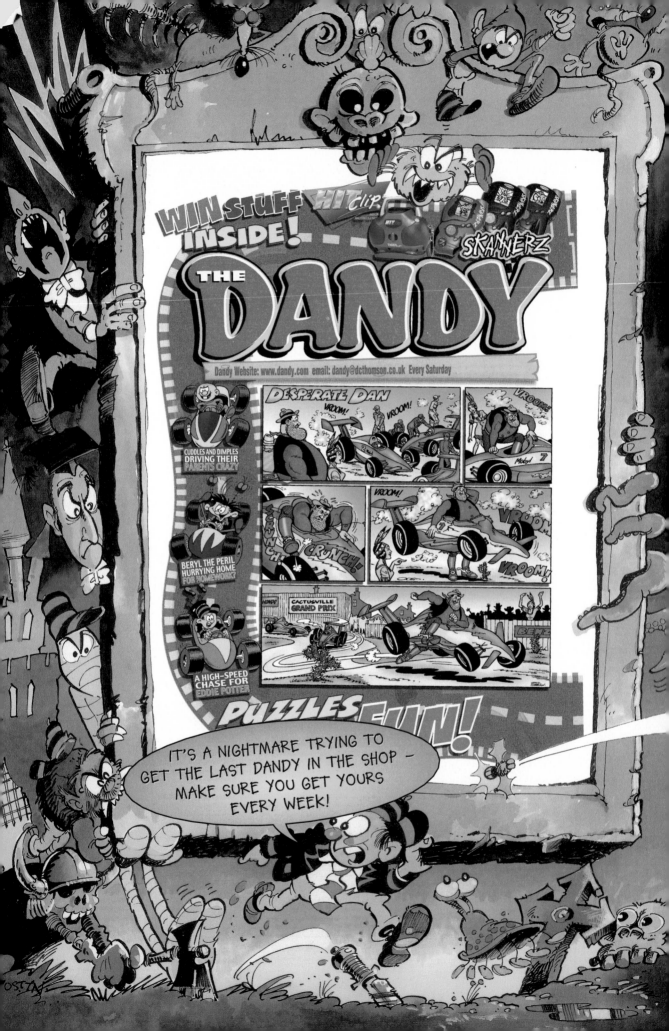

MARVO THE WONDERCHICKEN

and Henry Thrapplewhacker 49th

Hic! Hic!

Hic!

Hic!

CUDDLES and DIMPLES in "THE PILLOW CASE" PART 3

PERILOSAURUS

Pterosaurs were bat-like creatures which lived on Earth about 150 million years ago. Some species had wing spans of over 8m (26ft).

QUIZWORDS

1) Rest at night
2) Forest path
3) Bird of prey
4) Waterway
5) Eskimo shelter
6) Bang your feet
7) Large snake
8) Below
9) Baking powder
10) Footwear

Each answer has a letter from the word
PTEROSAURS

PTEROSAURS

HERE ARE 8 OF BERYL'S DRAWINGS.
WHICH 2 ARE EXACTLY THE SAME?

1

2

3

4

5

6

7

8

I'VE FOUND A DINOSAUR'S BONE!

I THINK IT WANTS IT BACK!

DAN/01-04
Gall & Strachan

Answers: Quizwords 1) SLEEP 2) TRAIL 3) EAGLE 4) RIVER 5) IGLOO 6) STAMP 7) COBRA 8) UNDER 9) FLOUR 10) SHOES. Beryl's Drawings 3 & 5 ARE IDENTICAL.

PUSS and BOOTS in HIGH JINKS!

HEE! HEE! GOT YOU THAT TIME.

ONE DAY YOU'LL GET YOURS, WILLY.

I FANCY A BURGER - BUT LOOK AT THE QUEUE.

I HATE QUEUES. WATCH THIS.

UGH! COUGH! GROO! THAT BURGER WAS BOWFIN'! YEEEUCH!

CHECK THIS.

HE MUST'VE HAD A BURGER FROM HERE.

THAT GOT RID OF THEM. TWO CHEESEBURGERS, PLEASE, AND HURRY.

YOU LITTLE WIND-UP MERCHANT.

YOU LOST ME CUSTOMERS! CLEAR OFF!

PHOOEY! HAVE YOU NO SENSE OF HUMOUR?